P9-CLR-648

Ðᴉꜱɴᴇʏ

THE WORLD OF

M@ANA

Featuring special concept art from the makers of Moana!

A special thanks to the wonderful people of the Pacific Islands
for inspiring us on this journey as we bring
the world of Moana to life.

Designed by Alfred Giuliani

Copyright © 2016 Disney Enterprises, Inc. All rights reserved.
Published in the United States by Random House Children's
Books, a division of Penguin Random House LLC, 1745 Broadway,
New York, NY 10019, and in Canada by Penguin Random House
Canada Limited, Toronto, in conjunction with Disney Enterprises,
Inc. Random House and the colophon are registered trademarks of
Penguin Random House LLC.

randomhousekids.com
ISBN 978-0-7364-3673-1
Printed in the United States of America
10 9 8 7 6 5 4 3 2 1

Random House Children's Books supports the First Amendment
and celebrates the right to read.

Disney

THE WORLD OF
M⊚ANA

By BILL SCOLLON

Random House 🏠 New York

Moana's World

Welcome to the world of Moana—a place of breathtaking beauty, rich in culture, traditions, and legends.

Moana lives in **Oceania**, in the Pacific Ocean, which is dotted with tens of thousands of islands. The islanders live in harmony with nature, drawing on the land and sea for everything they need.

North Pacific Ocean

RAWAKI

Tokelau

SAMOA

Mata-
litu

TONGA   MOTUNUI

Niue

TIKIRAU   TE KĀ

Impossible Cliff

0   200   400   600   800   1000   1200 Miles

PIHUKA

Tropic of Capricorn

The Edge of Nowhere

South Pacific Ocean

Moana's ancestors traveled across the water in mighty **voyaging canoes**. They started settlements on the new islands they found. The knowledge gained by the seafaring explorers helped make Moana's island home.

The Ocean

Moana and the other islanders have great **respect** for the ocean. They consider it a living, breathing thing with its own **feelings** and **moods**. It nourishes all life—from the tiniest barnacles found in tide pools to the monsters of the deep.

Ever since she was young, Moana has been drawn to the ocean. She didn't know that the ocean would bestow upon her a **gift** that would send her on a special **quest**.

The ocean is also the fabric that connects the islands. It is a highway for canoes, outriggers, and large sailing ships.

The Island of Motunui

The island of Motunui impressed Moana's ancestors the moment they laid eyes on it. It had **towering peaks** that could be seen for miles. Fresh water flowed down the sides of the mountains through a lush green forest.

But the most magnificent thing of all was the island's large bay, completely protected by a **coral reef**. It was the ideal place to build a village!

Motunui: Environment

Tucked safely inside the bay, the village of Motunui
blossomed. The islanders got most of their food and
resources from the **sea**. But they also grew fruits and
vegetables in the island's **mineral-rich soil**.

The land and sea provided **everything** the growing village needed. Motunui was a great place to live.

Motunui: Beaches

The beach was the villagers' front yard. The clear, cool water was a big part of their everyday life. Some of their favorite things to do were collecting seashells, watching colorful tropical fish dart back and forth, hunting for crabs, and dancing alongside the waves.

The villagers would launch their **fishing boats** and **great voyaging canoes** from the beach.

The Villagers

People lived happily on Motunui for a **thousand years**. The bustling village was home to farmers, fishermen, builders, clothing-makers, storytellers, musicians, and tattoo artists.

In ancient times, navigators—known as **wayfinders**—were among the most important inhabitants of any island society. Their ocean voyages expanded their knowledge of the world.

Whenever the fleet returned, villagers **paddled out** to greet them. The ships carried food, clothing, and other goods. And their crews brought back stories of adventure from beyond the reef.

The Villagers: The Chief and His Family

Moana's father, **Chief Tui**, rules Motunui. He and Moana's mother, **Sina**, look forward to the day their daughter will take Tui's place as the head of the island.

Motunui is a **peaceful** island. The chief has a very important job. He solves village issues, and he works to lift his community up.

The Villagers: Know Who You Are

On Motunui, villagers trust their chief and respect their elders. Moana's grandmother, **Gramma Tala**, taught Moana about the customs and beliefs of their people. She explained that it is important for every person to find out who they are meant to be. If they do, they will find their purpose in life and be happy.

The Villagers: Traditions and Legends

Storytellers like Gramma Tala help keep the culture alive by passing its legends and traditions on to each new generation. When Moana was little, she heard Gramma tell the story of **Maui, the demigod** who stole the heart of the mother island, Te Fiti. His actions caused a terrible darkness to spread across the world, which threatened the survival of Motunui!

The Village

When Moana's ancestors began building the village, they started by finding a special spot for the main gathering place, called the **Royal Marae.**

The homes of **villagers** came next. In Motunui, they stretched from the water's edge up into the hills overlooking the bay. Trees planted alongside the homes provided shade. A village architect oversaw the placement of all homes and gathering places. Once those were complete, the builders constructed a home for the chief in a central location, one that enhanced the chief's ability to rule and to host gatherings.

The Village: Fales

The islanders call their homes and meeting houses **fales**.
The sturdy buildings are often set on top of rock foundations
and are made from different kinds of wood, leaves, and
grasses. Strong rope woven from coconut fibers holds the
building material in place.

Royal Marae

Residences of the Chief's Relatives

Community (or Grand) Fale

Banyan Tree

Gramma's Fale

Chief's Fale

Cooking Fale

Boat Fale

Poles topped with **red feathers** ring one fale. That is Chief Tui's home. The striking red feathers signify **royalty**.

The Village: Clothing

Motunui's climate is **warm** all year long. The villagers wear clothes that are comfortable, yet functional. All garments are made from plant fibers, leaves, feathers, and shells.

The villagers like using **patterns** and decorating their outfits with fresh flowers. Accessories for special occasions, like ceremonies, are even more ornate, with impressive **headdresses** and bands for wrists, arms, and ankles.

The Village: Tapa

The islanders make a type of cloth called **tapa** from the inner bark of certain trees. First they soak the bark; then they beat it with mallets until the fibers get soft. Finally, the islanders pound layers of the fibers together until they become one big piece of fabric. Artisans use **natural dyes** to print geometric designs on the tapa.

U'a - Mulberry Tree

Tutua - Anvil

Pattern Made with Sticks

I'e - Tapa Beater

Upeti - Pattern Board

Faina - Small Knife

The Village: Accessories and Tattoos

The men and women of Motunui love to wear colorful **adornments**. Shells, seeds, dried beans, woven fibers, feathers, and other natural materials make for an endless variety of handcrafted accessories.

Tattoos are highly valued by the villagers. Each tattoo is sacred and full of meaning. They are a gift from the master tattoo artist. Gramma Tala has a **manta ray** tattooed across her back!

The Village: Animals

In addition to people, the village of Motunui is home to chickens and pigs. Most lead an active life, but a rooster named **Heihei** is well known for being completely absentminded.

Moana adopted a pig and named him **Pua**. The little pig is everyone's friend!

The Ocean:
Nature's Bounty

The villagers depend on the bounty of the sea. Fish and shellfish are not only a primary source of food, their bones and shells make everything from **belts** to **sewing needles**!

Every day, fishermen set nets out in the shallow bay. But over time, the fish population has gotten smaller and smaller. Moana wondered one day if the time had finally come to ask the chief for permission to sail **beyond the reef** and fish in the open ocean.

The Ocean: Beyond the Reef

The open ocean was a mystery to the people of Motunui. For a thousand years, every chief warned the people that the ocean was an unforgiving place full of mountainous **waves** and vicious **monsters**.

But Moana learned from Gramma Tala that her ancestors were voyagers who had traveled across the sea in great canoes. They felt **driven** to explore the world. It was who they **were**.

Moana felt the same irresistible call of the
ocean. She wanted to sail **beyond the reef**
and find out how far she could go.

The Wayfinders: Hidden Cavern

A hidden **lava tube** shrouded by vines led to a long-forgotten cavern. Inside were the remains of the **ancient fleet of voyaging boats**. There were canoes of all sizes, as well as outriggers and huge double-hulled sailing ships.

In a golden age of discovery, the ancient wayfinders had traveled vast distances and back again using only **natural signs**, without any navigational instruments.

Wayfinding

Wayfinding is the skill of using the sun, moon, stars, winds, currents, and other elements of nature to **navigate** hundreds of miles of open ocean.

Wayfinders led the expeditions that mapped islands, found new trading partners, or started new settlements. Something **inside** Moana told her that one day, she could become a wayfinder.

The Wayfinders: The Ships, the Journeys

The great voyaging ships explored the ocean until **Maui** stole the **heart of Te Fiti** and a darkness moved through the sea and across islands. Soon, the ships stopped returning.

No one knew what had happened to them, but Motunui's chief decided he had to act. To protect his people, the chief **forbade** all travel beyond the reef.

Moana's Canoe

Moana took to the sea in one of the canoes from the hidden cavern. Built for ocean travel, it had a **closed deck** to keep the boat from getting swamped. Wooden panels stitched together made the double-hulled craft very sturdy. Ropes woven from coconut fibers controlled the single sail.

Moana had little sailing experience when she left Motunui. But above her was the same **blanket of stars** her ancestors had used to find their way.

Maui's Island: Maui, the Fallen Demigod

A violent storm sent Moana crashing onto the beach of a barren, rocky island.

It was the island of **Maui** the demigod.
He'd been stuck there since losing his
magic fishhook, the source of all
his power. Maui was full of bravado
and loved boasting about his exploits.
Moana didn't like his bluster, but the truth
was that Maui had a big heart—and a big **secret**.

Maui's Tattoos

Tattoos covered Maui from head to foot. Each one meant something special. Many of them represented his great **feats**—like pushing up the sky, lassoing the sun, pulling up islands, and battling monsters!

One of his tattoos was **magical**. It was a small picture of Maui that could come to life. Though he couldn't talk, **Mini Maui** used gestures and pantomime to try to get the real Maui to do the right thing!

Maui's Island: Maui the Shape-Shifter

Maui's magical fishhook was given to him by the gods.
The hook had incredible **powers**. Not only did it make
Maui unbelievably strong, it gave him the ability to
turn into different creatures.

Maui was a **shape-shifter**. He could become
a hawk, a lizard, a shark, or many other
creatures—as long as he had the fishhook.

But the hook was at the bottom of the sea. To get it back, Maui needed a **canoe**.

The Kakamora!

The Kakamora were a tribe of **scavengers** who would stop at nothing to get what they wanted. They sailed on floating islands made of driftwood, coconut shells, and whatever else they could find.

The Kakamora communicated by **drumming**. Dressed in their coconut armor, the pint-sized bandits didn't look very threatening. But **nothing** was further from the truth!

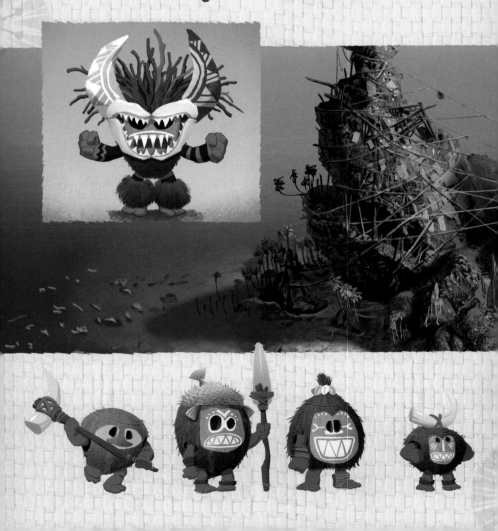

The Kakamora: Attack!

The Kakamora were ruthless **pirates**! They
prepared for battle by painting on war faces.
Clever and skilled, the pirates began an
attack by spearing their target and
reeling it in with ropes. Then warriors
slid down the ropes to board their victims'
boat and steal everything they could.

Their tactics usually meant a swift
victory, but they'd never faced
Moana and Maui before!

Monsters

The Kakamora weren't the only brutes who roamed
Oceania. It was home to monsters of every size and
description—ravenous giant **eels**, ill-tempered **clams**,
and predatory **fish**.

But the majority of the monsters
lurked far beneath the ocean, from eight-eyed
bats to enormous **crabs** who loved anything shiny.

Gateway to the Realm of Monsters: The Impossible Cliff

Of all the volcanic islands, none matched the awe-inspiring heights of the vertical peak known as the **Impossible Cliff**. After pounding open the entrance, Moana and Maui dove straight down into a swirling whirlpool!

It was the entrance to a mythological place called **the realm of monsters**—the unseen realm that existed in a world under the ocean.

Lalotai

Lalotai was a fantastical place. The **luminescent**
world was lit by glowing plants, giant anemone trees,
and sea urchin spires. Monsters of all kinds crawled,
slithered, or flew through the shadows.

Moana and Maui carefully
made their way past geysers
and over narrow rock bridges
to find the lair of the villainous
Tamatoa.

Tamatoa

A monstrous crab named **Tamatoa** ruled Lalotai.
He was a collector of just about everything—especially
if it was valuable and shiny. His lair overflowed with
riches. But there was one treasure he had that Maui
couldn't do without—Maui's **fishhook**.

Te Kā

The Pacific Islands were home to **volcanoes**. After all,
volcanoes had built most of the islands in the first place. But
the volcanic barrier islands that guarded Te Fiti were different.
They were the home of **Te Kā**, a demon of earth and fire.

Te Kā's billowing smoke, hot lava, and flying boulders were no match for Moana's bravery and determination. Getting the best of Te Kā brought Moana face to face with her **destiny**.

Te Fiti

Moana returned the heart of **Te Fiti**, and the **mother island** was restored. From her heart came all life. Te Fiti blossomed, and the darkness that threatened every island retreated from Oceania.

For the people of Motunui, there was no longer a reason to fear traveling beyond the reef.

The New Wayfinders

Moana, now a skilled wayfinder, navigated her way back home by reading the wind, the ocean currents, and the stars.

The island of Motunui bloomed with full health once more. Chief Tui and Sina, brimming with pride, ran to the shore to welcome their daughter home.

Moana the wayfinder went on to lead her people into a new age of voyaging!

Fox
Makes Friends

O9-BUD-729

No part of this publication may be reproduced, stored in a retrieval system, or transmitted in any form or by any means, electronic, mechanical, photocopying, recording, or otherwise, without written permission of the publisher. For information regarding permission, write to Sterling Publishing Company, Inc., 387 Park Avenue South, New York, NY 10016.

ISBN-13: 978-0-439-89881-2

ISBN-10: 0-439-89881-1

Copyright © 2005 by Adam Relf. All rights reserved.
Published by Scholastic Inc., 557 Broadway, New York, NY 10012,
by arrangement with Sterling Publishing Company, Inc.
SCHOLASTIC and associated logos are trademarks and/or
registered trademarks of Scholastic Inc.

12 11 10 9 8 7 6 5 4 3 2 1   6 7 8 9 10 11/0

Printed in the U.S.A.   40

First Scholastic printing, September 2006

Fox
Makes Friends

Adam Relf

SCHOLASTIC INC.
New York Toronto London Auckland Sydney
Mexico City New Delhi Hong Kong Buenos Aires

Fox sat in his room.
He was bored.
"I know," he said.
"I need a friend."

Fox picked up his net and went to see his mom.
"I'm going to catch a friend," he declared.
"You can't catch friends," Mom explained.
"You have to *make* friends."
So Fox put down his net and
set off to make a friend.

"What can I make a friend out of?"
he thought.
He picked up some sticks, an apple, and
some nuts and fixed them all together.
At last he had a brand new friend
standing in front of him.

"Are you my friend?" Fox asked,
but the friend said nothing.
"Can you come and play?" he said,
but the friend didn't move. "Maybe he's
too small," Fox thought. "I need to make
a bigger friend!"

Just then a rabbit ran by.
"Excuse me," said Fox. "I'm trying
to make a friend but this one is
too small. Can you help me
make a bigger one?"
     "Okay," said Rabbit.

They worked together and picked up a turnip,
some tomatoes, and some twigs. They stuck them
all together and had a bigger friend
standing before them.
"Will you be our friend?" they asked,
but there was no answer.

"Can you come and play?" they said, but the friend just stood there. "Maybe he's still too small," said Rabbit.

A moment later Fox and Rabbit
heard giggling in the treetops.
It was a squirrel.
"What a mess you two are
making!" he laughed.
"Well, if you can do
better, come down and
help us!" said Fox.
"Okay," said Squirrel.

This time all three of them set to work.
They picked a huge pumpkin, a turnip,
some branches, and some apples.
They put them all together and had
the biggest friend they could make.
"Are you our friend?" they asked.
"Please can you come and play?"
But there was no reply.

Finally they all gave up.
"Oh, well," said Fox. "I suppose I will
never be able to make a friend."

Just then Fox's mother
came by.
"Hello," she said. "Who are
all your new friends?"
"Oh," said Fox. "My plan
didn't work. We made friends
but they won't play with us."
"Not them!" giggled his mother.
"These friends!" she said,
pointing to Squirrel
and Rabbit.

Fox looked over at Squirrel and
Rabbit and suddenly realized
that he had been making
friends all along!

So Fox, Squirrel, and Rabbit played for the rest of the day, and they stayed friends forever.